Bunch

TO FAME

by Nancy K. Wallace
illustrated by Amanda Chronister

magic
wagon

visit us at www.abdopublishing.com

For my husband, Dennie, and my original Book Bunch: Hanna, Derrick, &
Dakota —NW

Published by Magic Wagon, a division of the ABDO Group,
PO Box 398166, Minneapolis, MN 55439. Copyright © 2013 by Abdo
Consulting Group, Inc. International copyrights reserved in all countries.
All rights reserved. No part of this book may be reproduced in any form
without written permission from the publisher.

Calico Chapter Books™ is a trademark and logo of Magic Wagon.

Printed in the United States of America, North Mankato, Minnesota.
102012
012013
This book contains at least 10% recycled materials.

Text by Nancy K. Wallace
Illustrations by Amanda Chronister
Edited by Stephanie Hedlund and Rochelle Baltzer
Layout and design by Neil Klinepier

Library of Congress Cataloging-in-Publication Data
Wallace, Nancy K.
  Claim to fame / by Nancy K. Wallace ; illustrated by Amanda Chronister.
    p. cm. -- (Abby and the Book Bunch)
  Summary: Summer is almost gone, and third-grader Abby Spencer and
her friends, the Book Bunch, are spending their time working on a play for
the local public library, and visiting Abigail Flynn at the Evergreen Nursing
Home.
  ISBN 978-1-61641-912-7
1. Volunteers--Juvenile fiction. 2. Public libraries--Juvenile fiction. 3.
Books and reading--Juvenile fiction. 4. Children's plays--Juvenile fiction.
5. Nursing homes--Juvenile fiction. [1. Voluntarism--Fiction. 2. Public
libraries--Fiction. 3. Books and reading--Fiction. 4. Plays--Fiction. 5.
Nursing homes--Fiction.] I. Chronister, Amanda, ill. II. Title.
  PZ7.W158752Cl 2013
  813.6--dc23
                                      2012029413

CONTENTS

Glue Sticks and Glitter

"I'm scared to be in the library play," Abby said.

Abby's best friend, Sydney, stopped and sat down on the top of Evergreen Library's steps. She squinted at her friend in the bright summer sunlight.

"I am too," she admitted. "I've never had a speaking part in a play before."

"Me either," Abby replied. She sat down and tapped her sandal on the sidewalk. "I'm afraid I'll forget my lines."

"You're the narrator," Sydney said. "You have the biggest part."

"And you're the princess," Abby reminded her. "Your part is big, too."

Sydney sighed. "We'll just have to practice a lot."

Abby's foot tapped faster. "I'm afraid I'll forget even if I do practice a lot," she said.

Sydney frowned. "Maybe we should just tell Mrs. Mackenzie we can't do it. She wouldn't want us to worry about it."

Abby groaned. "I don't want to disappoint her. She's really excited about this play. It's the main event for the Summer Reading Finale!"

Abby and Sydney's third grade class

had volunteered as Community Helpers for a month. Ever since then, Abby and her friends had continued to volunteer at the library. The children's librarian, Mrs. Mackenzie, called them Abby and the Book Bunch because they helped her all the time.

All of a sudden the library door swung open with a bang. "Look out!" Abby shouted.

Two little boys ran out of the library. They waved glittery kites with long paper tails.

Sydney ducked as a kite tail tangled in her blond hair. Abby quickly pulled the sticky paper free.

The boys ran off giggling. Their mom hurried after them. "Slow down!" she yelled.

Sydney shook her head to straighten her hair. "Thanks for warning me," she said.

Abby brushed at Sydney's shoulder. "There is glitter all over you!" she said with a giggle. "You look just like Mrs. Mackenzie."

Sydney laughed. Mrs. Mackenzie always seemed to be covered with glitter. "I'll bet there will be a mess to clean up after Story Time!" she said.

"I don't mind," said Abby.

Abby returned four books to the circulation desk as they went in. A trail of glitter and paper scraps led to the Children's Area. Two folding tables were buried in craft supplies. A toddler sat under one of the tables rubbing a glue stick on his stomach.

Sydney made a face. "Yuck!" she said. "You get Trevor. I'll get the trash can."

Abby grabbed a toy and knelt down beside the little boy. "Hi, Trevor!" she said. "Do you want to come out and play with this train?"

Trevor held out the grimy glue stick. "Goo," he said.

Abby took the glue stick. "Let's trade," she said, pushing the engine under the table.

Trevor beamed. He reached for the train and the glue stick. "Goo train," he giggled.

"No more glue," Abby said. "The glue is all gone." She slid out from under the table and set the glue stick safely in its box.

Mrs. Mackenzie appeared, holding a crying child in her arms. Glitter twinkled on her face and hair. "Thank you, Abby!" she gasped. "Some of the mothers are late picking their kids up. Trevor has been gluing everything in sight."

Trevor smacked the train into the table leg. A shower of glitter rained down on the carpet like snow. Sydney arrived just in time with the trash can.

Abby pointed at the paper on the table. "Do we need to save any of this for another program?" she asked.

Mrs. Mackenzie shook her head. Glitter drifted through the air all around her. "No," she said. "Just dump it all into the recycle bin. There is nothing I want to save."

Abby and Sydney cleared off the table. They had to be careful not to step on Trevor.

"Did you say anything about the play to Mrs. Mackenzie?" Sydney whispered.

"No," Abby whispered. "She's so busy. Maybe we can talk to her later."

"We can't wait too long," Sydney warned. "It will be too late! The play is only two weeks away!"

"I know," Abby said miserably. They had been so excited when Mrs. Mackenzie had first asked them to be in the play.

They had all wanted to be in it! Now it seemed scary to have to remember all those lines in front of an audience.

Sydney leaned closer. "Zachary is scared, too," she said.

Abby made a face. "Why is he scared? He's the king," she said. "He only has one line."

Sydney laughed. "At least Dakota isn't nervous," she said. "He loves being the frog."

"He'll do anything," Abby agreed.

Sydney laughed. "I have an idea! Maybe Dakota would like to play all the parts. Then we could just sit and watch!"

Abby giggled. "That would be funny," she said. She could just imagine Dakota racing back and forth to change costumes. *That would be hard to do,* Abby thought. *But it might be easier than telling Mrs. Mackenzie that we don't want to be in the play.*

Pool Pranks

I love summer! Abby thought as she circled Evergreen's community pool. She glided smoothly through the cool water. Kids laughed and screeched all around her. The sun glittered on the water. The air smelled like sunscreen and chlorine.

Everything was perfect except for one thing. The library play lurked unpleasantly in the back of her mind. Abby flipped onto her back and floated in the water. She tried to rehearse her lines in her head. But the words drifted away like smoke.

A beach ball splashed down right in Abby's face. "Hey!" she protested as she stood up.

Dakota popped out of the water beside her. He grinned and grabbed the ball. "Thanks for finding my ball!" he said.

"Well, no thanks for throwing it in my face!" said Abby. She rubbed her nose. "Why don't you and Zachary play ball over there. Let Sydney and me swim!"

Dakota pointed to a beach towel on the deck. "Sydney's working on her tan!"

said Dakota. "I was just trying to keep you company."

Abby looked over at Sydney stretched out in the sun. "When did she get out of the water?" she asked.

"About five minutes ago," said Dakota. "You must have been swimming in your sleep!"

Abby shook her head. Her hair dripped in her face and on her shoulders. "No," she said, "I was just thinking about how much I love summer! It's nice not to have school for a while."

"I thought you liked school," said Dakota.

Abby grinned. "I do, but I like sleeping, too!"

"And swimming," said Dakota.

Abby nodded. "And swimming!" she agreed.

"My dad's grilling tonight," said Dakota. "He said I could have some friends over. Sydney's coming. Do you want to come, too?"

"I can't," Abby said. "I promised Abigail Flynn that I would visit her tonight. Gram is going to drop me off while she does some shopping."

Dakota wiggled his eyebrows. "You'll have more fun at my house," he said.

"I like to go to Evergreen Nursing Home," said Abby. "I think things are kind of boring there. Abigail is always so glad to see me! I want to take her some of the pink roses from the bushes by the playhouse."

Abigail Flynn used to live on the same block where Abby lived. The playhouse Abigail had when she was little was still in Abby's backyard. Abby's dad had fixed it up this spring. Abby and her mom had planted rose bushes around it.

"Hey!" yelled Zachary from across the pool. "Are you playing or not?"

Dakota launched the beach ball at Zachary's head. "Gotta go," he said.

Abby laughed and swam over to the ladder. She climbed out of the pool and grabbed her beach towel. Sydney was lying on her towel with a magazine over her face.

"Bug off, Zachary!" Sydney snarled. "You're dripping all over me!"

"Sorry!" said Abby, jumping back.

Sydney tipped her magazine back and squinted up at Abby. "I didn't know it was you," she said. "Zachary is being a real pain! First he got my magazine all wet. Then, he stuck gum on my toenail!"

Abby gasped. The tips of Sydney's beautiful blond hair were bright pink!

Sydney sat up. "What's the matter?" she said. "What are you staring at?"

"Your hair is pink!" said Abby.

"It's what?" screamed Sydney.

Abby stared at Sydney. "Your hair is bright pink!" she repeated.

Abby could hear Zachary and Dakota laughing. They were splashing water and howling.

Sydney jumped to her feet. "That's not funny!" she yelled. "You two are in big trouble!"

"It's only Kool-Aid!" Zachary snickered. "It will wash right out."

"It better wash out!" snapped Sydney. She stamped her foot and looked at Abby. "I am so mad!"

Abby shoved their towels in their bags. "Come on," she said. "I'll help you wash it in the sink in the restroom."

"What if it doesn't come out?" Sydney wailed.

Abby gulped. She didn't even want to think about what would happen if the color didn't come out. "It'll be fine," she said soothingly. "Let's hurry."

"I hate boys!" snapped Sydney. She turned around and looked at Dakota. "And I'm not coming to your house tonight, either!"

Dakota threw his hands in the air. "Fine!" he shouted. "Don't come!"

Abby patted Sydney's shoulder. "Do you want to come with me to visit Abigail?" she asked.

"Sure," Sydney sniffed. "I just don't want to be around Dakota or Zachary!"

Tickled Pink

Abigail Flynn was waiting when Abby and Sydney arrived at the nursing home. This week they had so much to tell her!

"It sounds as though you girls have had a bad week," Abigail said. "You were already worried about the library play. And then the boys put Kool-Aid on Sydney's hair."

Sydney folded her arms over her chest. "I will never speak to Dakota or Zachary again!" she said.

Abigail adjusted her glasses and leaned forward in her wheelchair. "Never is a long time," she said. She peered at the blue baseball cap that was hiding Sydney's hair. "Is it really pink?" asked Abigail. "I want see it!"

Abby nodded. "It's really, really pink," she said, patting her friend's hand. "It's bright pink!"

"Really bright pink," agreed Sydney. "But they just dyed the ends of it."

"This is the most exciting thing that has happened in months!" said Abigail. "I've never seen anyone with pink hair. Please take your hat off, Sydney."

"I don't want to," Sydney said.

"Please," coaxed Abigail. "Old ladies don't have much excitement in their lives."

Sydney rolled her eyes. She glanced behind them to see if anyone was in the hall. "Can I close the door first?" she asked.

"Of course," said Abigail, grinning. "And turn the top light on. I want the full effect."

"Okay," said Sydney. "But you have to promise not to laugh. And you can't take pictures or anything!"

"I don't even own a camera, dear," Abigail said solemnly.

"I'll get the light," said Abby. She waited until Sydney shut the door to flick the switch.

Sydney stood in the center of Abigail's room. She pulled her hat off in one quick motion. Her hair cascaded down over her shoulders. It was a silky blond waterfall with bright pink ends.

Abigail gasped. "Oh my," she said. "I wonder what flavor they used."

"It was strawberry," said Sydney. "They sprinkled the powder on my hair when it was wet from swimming."

"Her hair still smells like strawberries," Abby added.

"I love the smell of strawberries," said Abigail. "They smell just like summer. And I think your hair looks beautiful! You look just like a fairy princess!"

Sydney blushed. "Really?" she asked.

"It is kind of cute," said Abby.

"It can be your claim to fame, Sydney!" Abigail said.

"What's a claim to fame?" asked Sydney.

"It's something special," said Abigail. "It's something that sets you apart from everyone else."

Sydney shook her head. "I don't think I want my claim to fame to be pink hair," she said. "I think this color will look awful with my favorite T-shirt."

"Would you like purple better?" asked Abigail. "You could use grape Kool-Aid!"

Abby giggled. "Blueberry would match your eyes," she said.

Abigail chuckled. "You could try that next. Use a different flavor every month!"

"That might be fun," Sydney giggled. "But I don't want to dye my hair! Those boys make me so mad!"

"Maybe you should dye the boys' hair," Abigail suggested.

"They have brown hair," said Sydney. "I don't think it would work as well."

"Your hair was perfect because it is so light," said Abby.

Abigail suddenly said, "I have a wonderful idea! Could you girls dye my hair pink?"

Abby and Sydney stopped laughing. They looked at each other and then at Abigail.

"My hair is white," said Abigail. "It would be beautiful pink! Could you buy some strawberry Kool-Aid for me?"

Abby cleared her throat. "Abigail, I don't think that's a good idea," she said. "What would the nurses think?"

Abigail waved a hand in the air. "I don't care what they think! I'm 100 years old. If I want pink hair it's nobody's business. It's not as though I have to ask my parents!"

"Won't you feel funny?" asked Sydney. "No one else here has pink hair."

"That's the point," said Abigail. "Everything here is the same. I want to do something different. I'm tired of mashed potatoes every Thursday night and bingo every Tuesday. Will you help me dye my hair?"

Abby looked at Sydney. They both nodded slowly.

"All right then," said Abigail. "You help me with my hair and I'll help you learn your lines for your play. How would that be?"

Sydney and Abby grinned. "That would be great!" they said.

Shortages

Sydney and Abby piled into the car outside Evergreen Nursing Home. Abby pushed some packages into the middle of the backseat. She buckled her seat belt.

Gram turned and smiled at them. "How was Abigail?" she asked as she pulled away from the curb.

"She was very happy to see us," said Abby. She thought about dying Abigail's hair. Her heart beat a little faster. "I think we should visit her more often."

"I can take you again later this week," Gram offered.

"Thanks," said Abby. "Abigail will love that!"

"She even liked my hair!" Sydney added.

Gram laughed. "I haven't even seen your hair yet. Will you show it to me?"

Sydney adjusted her ball cap. She glanced at Abby. "Maybe later," she replied.

Abby leaned forward. "Did you already go to the grocery store, Gram?" she asked.

Gram shook her head. "No, I still need to stop on the way home. Is there something you need?"

Abby's stomach did a flip-flop. "Could we get a package of strawberry Kool-Aid?" she asked.

Gram laughed. "I thought you didn't ever want to have Kool-Aid again!"

Abby cleared her throat. "Strawberry is still our favorite flavor," she said. "We just don't want to have it in our hair."

"Okay," said Gram. She turned into the parking lot at the Stop and Shop. "I have to get some hamburger buns for your mother, Abby. You girls can go and get the Kool-Aid. I'll meet you at the checkout."

Abby and Sydney raced down the snack aisle. They stopped by the shelves of Kool-Aid.

Abby looked at the different flavors. "There are only two packages of strawberry left," she said.

Sydney rolled her eyes. "The boys probably brought the rest," she said. "We'd better buy both packages."

Abby grabbed the packages and headed for the checkout. Gram was waiting. She had a dozen hamburger buns and a gallon of milk. Abby's hands shook as she put the Kool-Aid down for the clerk. She couldn't believe they were really going to dye Abigail's hair pink!

As soon as they pulled into the driveway at home, Abby's golden retriever, Lucy, greeted them. Lucy gave both girls sloppy kisses.

Abby's dad had lit the grill. "I heard you girls missed out on a picnic at Dakota's," he said. "Your mom made some baked beans and potato salad. We can have a picnic right here."

"That sounds yummy!" said Abby.

Abby's dad looked at Sydney. "Is there any chance I can see your famous hair?" he asked.

Sydney looked down at the porch floor. "I don't know," she said.

Abby's dad grinned. "Well, think about it. It sure sounds gorgeous to me!"

Sydney hesitated. "I guess you can see it," she said, taking off her hat.

"Wow!" said Abby's dad, gesturing with the spatula. "You look beautiful, Sydney! You should put your baseball cap away and show off that pink hair!"

Sydney blushed, but she didn't put her hat back on.

Abby reached for the grocery bag. "I'll carry that in, Gram," she offered. She wanted to take the Kool-Aid out and hide it in her bedroom.

Gram pointed at the red checked tablecloth and silverware lying on a chair. "Why don't you set the table," Gram suggested. "I'll take care of this."

Abby glanced at Sydney. "Okay," she said.

Abby and Sydney set the table quickly and ran inside. The kitchen smelled liked a picnic. There were deviled eggs and chocolate cupcakes on the table!

"We thought we'd cheer you girls up!" said Abby's mom.

"Thanks!" said Abby and Sydney. Abby looked everywhere for the grocery bag but didn't see it.

Abby's mom handed Abby a plate with the hamburgers on it. "Can you take this out to your dad?" she asked.

Gram turned from the sink and held out a huge pitcher of strawberry Kool-

Aid. "And you can carry the Kool-Aid, Sydney," she said with a smile. "I made both packages since you girls asked for it specially."

Abby gulped. The last two packages of strawberry Kool-Aid at the Stop and Shop were gone! What would they do now?

Disappointments

Abby and Sydney walked slowly down the hall at Evergreen Nursing Home. Abigail Flynn had promised to help them practice their lines for the play today. They had planned to give her the strawberry Kool-Aid, but it was all gone.

"I feel bad," said Abby.

"Me too," said Sydney. "But it wasn't our fault."

"I know," said Abby. "Gram didn't know what we were going to do with the Kool-Aid. She just thought we wanted to drink it."

"Well, that is what you usually do with Kool-Aid," Sydney agreed. "I'll ask my mom to look for strawberry the next time she goes to the store."

"Okay," said Abby. "I just hate to disappoint Abigail. I hope she won't be upset."

The door to Abigail Flynn's room was wide open. Sunshine streamed through the big windows. Abigail sat looking out at the flowers on the patio. She turned her wheelchair around when the girls walked in.

"There you are!" Abigail said, holding out her hands to greet them. "I have been looking forward to your visit all week!"

Abby looked down. Her sandal went *tap, tap, tap* on the floor.

"What's the matter?" Abigail asked in concern.

"We bought the last two packages of strawberry Kool-Aid at the Stop and Shop," Abby explained.

"Wonderful!" Abigail said, clapping her hands. "Can you dye my hair today?"

Abby got tears in her eyes. "But we don't have the Kool-Aid anymore, Abigail. We didn't tell Gram why we bought it, and she made it for our picnic last week!"

"Did everyone drink it?" Abigail asked with a giggle.

Abby and Sydney nodded.

Abigail patted Abby's hand. "Don't worry, dear," she said. "The Stop and Shop will get more Kool-Aid. I'm sure they sell a lot of it over the summer!"

"They do," said Abby.

"You could try a different color," Sydney suggested. "They were only sold out of strawberry."

Abigail shook her head. "I have my heart set on pink," she said. "I can't wait to see the expression on Gertrude Smith's face when I come to play bingo with pink hair!"

Abby giggled. "I would like to see that, too!" she said.

"Me too!" said Sydney.

"I will be the talk of Evergreen Nursing Home. My pink hair will be my claim to fame!" Abigail laughed. "Now how is your play coming along? Did you bring your scripts?"

"We're still not very good," said Sydney. "We remember our lines when we say them to each other. But when anyone else is listening, we get nervous."

Abigail patted the bed next to her. "Come and sit down beside me. I'll be glad to help you!"

"I just wish we didn't have to stand in front of all those people," Abby said.

"Remember that a lot of those people will be your friends and families," said Abigail. "They will be very proud of you!"

"It's still scary," said Abby.

Abigail squeezed her hand. "I'm sure your play will be wonderful!" she said. "I just wish I could see it."

Wednesday Worries

Abby was ready early Wednesday morning. She and Sydney were going to the library to help Mrs. Mackenzie. Then, the phone rang.

"I'll get it!" Abby cried. She picked up the phone and said, "Hello!"

"Hi," said Sydney.

"Hi," said Abby. "Do you need a ride to the library?"

"I can't go," said Sydney. "That's why I called. My mom is helping Pastor Elizabeth clean the kitchen cupboards at the church. She says I have to help."

"Yuck!" said Abby.

"Double yuck!" said Sydney. "And guess what. My mom bought me a T-shirt to match my hair."

Abby smiled. "That's awesome!" she said.

"Do you want to come over this afternoon when I get home?" asked Sydney. "I can show you my new shirt."

"Sure," said Abby. "I'll see you later."

Gram dropped Abby off at the library. Mrs. Mackenzie had just finished a kindergarten program. There was a lot to clean up!

Abby picked up scissors and paper. She wiped off sticky tables and glue bottles. Finally, she collected the last two puppets from the window seat in the Children's Area. She carried the frog and toad into Mrs. Mackenzie's office.

"Where should I put these?" Abby asked.

Mrs. Mackenzie turned around. She was holding a box of craft supplies. A monkey puppet hung over one of her shoulders. A snake puppet dangled from one hand.

"Just put them on my desk," she said with a smile.

Abby glanced at Mrs. Mackenzie's desk. Stacks of paper towered unsteadily. Cans of glitter, paint, and pipe cleaners tipped near the edge. Two boxes were piled on top of the phone.

"Maybe I could put them in the cupboard in the back," Abby suggested. "Do you need them again this week?"

Mrs. Mackenzie thought for a moment. "No, I don't," she said. "I think we are done with the puppets. I can't believe the Summer Reading Program is almost over!"

A familiar feeling of dread settled over Abby. That meant the play was soon, too.

Mrs. Mackenzie perched the monkey puppet on her desk chair and hung the snake on the doorknob. "Could you take these puppets to the back?" she asked.

"Sure," said Abby. She picked up the other two puppets. The monkey was her favorite. Its fur felt warm and comforting. She squeezed it against her chest.

Mrs. Mackenzie gave her a long look. "Is something the matter, Abby?" she asked.

Abby hesitated. She had to tell Mrs. Mackenzie that she and Sydney were worried about the play.

"Sydney and I are afraid we'll forget our lines in the play," she finally stammered.

Mrs. Mackenzie gave her a reassuring smile. "You are doing very well at rehearsal," she said.

"It's not the same as doing it in front of an audience," said Abby. "There are going to be a lot of people there!"

Mrs. Mackenzie sat down in her chair. She folded her hands in front of her. "What can I do to help?" she asked.

Abby looked at the floor. She couldn't suggest canceling the play. There had to be another way.

"I don't know," she said.

Mrs. Mackenzie smiled and patted Abby's shoulder. "We'll make sure you get lots of practice," she said. "And I'll have a script backstage. I can always help you if you forget your lines."

"Okay," said Abby. She turned toward the door with the puppets in her arms.

"Please don't worry," Mrs. Mackenzie called after her.

"Don't worry," Abby repeated quietly as she walked to the back of the library.

"Don't worry," she said again as she unlocked the cupboard door.

Abby tucked the frog and toad beside the princess puppet. She put the monkey next to the king puppet. She patted the puppets and locked the cupboard door.

"Don't worry," Abby said a third time. She just wished that saying something could make it come true!

Trash and Treasure

Gram dropped Abby off at Sydney's house when she was finished at the library. Sydney was sitting on her front porch. She ran down the sidewalk to meet Abby.

"I am so glad you're here!" Sydney said. Her eyes twinkled. She put her hand on Abby's arm. Her voice lowered to a whisper. "You'll never guess what I found at church."

"What did you find?" asked Abby.

Just then, Sydney's mom opened the door. "Hi, Abby," she said.

"Hi, Mrs. Thomas!" said Abby.

"Lunch is ready," Mrs. Thomas said. "Why don't you girls come in the kitchen?"

Sydney pushed Abby down the hall in front of her.

Abby squirmed around to look at Sydney. "What did you find?" she asked again.

Sydney put her hands behind her back. "I'll tell you later," she whispered.

Sydney's mom had made bacon, lettuce, and tomato sandwiches for lunch. She poured them big glasses of lemonade.

"This is the first ripe tomato from our garden," Sydney said.

Abby took a big bite of her sandwich. The bacon was extra crispy and the tomato was juicy.

"Our tomatoes aren't ready yet," said Abby. "Gram goes out to check on them about six times a day. My dad says he's going to paint one red just to fool her."

"That would be mean," said Mrs. Thomas.

Sydney giggled. "What if she ate it?"

Abby took a big gulp of lemonade. The ice cubes clinked in her glass when she set it down.

"My dad thinks it's funny to play tricks on people," Abby said. "Once he froze a plastic bug in an ice cube. Then, he put it in my mom's lemonade."

"Yuck!" said Sydney's mom. "That would be awful!"

Sydney held out a strand of her hair and wiggled the end. "Maybe all boys like to play tricks," she said.

"Maybe," said Abby. "But your new shirt looks awesome with your hair!"

Sydney grinned. "Thanks," she said. "I still wish we could play a really mean trick on the boys."

Abby shook her head. "I don't think that's a good idea. They would just do something else to us and it would never end."

"I think Abby's right," said Sydney's mom. "Who knows what the boys would do next!"

"Dakota came in to help at the library this morning," said Abby. "I told him your hair was still pink. He and Zachary thought the Kool-Aid would wash right out. Dakota said he was sorry."

Sydney's eyes narrowed. "Was he the one who did it?" she asked.

"He didn't say," said Abby. "And I didn't ask him." She finished the last bite of her sandwich. She couldn't wait to know what Sydney had found at the church.

"Please don't worry," said Sydney's mom. "Your hair will be back to normal after we wash it a few more times. I'm sure the boys will never do it again."

"Well, I'm still not speaking to either of them!" Sydney said.

"They are both in the play," Abby reminded her.

Sydney sighed. "I guess I'll have to speak to them, then," she said. She picked up her plate and put it in the dishwasher. "Why don't we go practice our lines, Abby?"

"Sure," said Abby, sliding her plate in next to Sydney's. "Thank you for lunch, Mrs. Thomas."

"Thanks, Mom," said Sydney.

"You're welcome, girls," said Mrs. Thomas. "Have fun with your art project."

Abby looked at Sydney. "What art project?" she whispered.

Sydney shook her head. "Come up to my room," she said mysteriously.

The girls ran up the stairs to Sydney's room. Sydney closed the door behind them and picked up a bag off her bed. "Look at what Pastor Elizabeth was throwing away," she said.

Sydney dumped ten packages of Kool-Aid on the bed. They were all different flavors! And two packages were strawberry!

"That's awesome!" said Abby. "Why did she throw them out?"

"They were in the back of one of the cupboards. And they are all expired!" Sydney said. "I asked if I could have them."

Abby gasped. "What did she say?"

Sydney laughed. "I told her we needed them for a kind of art project. Pastor Elizabeth told me to have fun and to remember not to drink them!"

Abby giggled. "Well, it is sort of an art project," she said.

Sydney grinned. "That's

what I thought," she agreed. "It's kind of like painting."

"I don't know," said Abby. "I can't believe we're doing this. What do you think Abigail will look like with pink hair?"

"I guess we're going to find out!" said Sydney. "When can Gram take us to Evergreen Nursing Home?"

Sweet Dreams

It was Friday afternoon before Gram could drive Abby and Sydney to Evergreen Nursing Home again. The girls stuffed the packages of Kool-Aid in the pockets of their shorts before they went out to the car.

"Why are we taking all of the Kool-Aid?" Abby asked.

"So Abigail has a choice," said Sydney. "Maybe she won't want strawberry hair when she sees how long the color lasts."

Abby was worried. "What if Gram asks what is in our pockets?" she asked Sydney.

Sydney shrugged. "She's not going to ask."

Abby hung back. "But what if she does?" she asked. "What should I say?"

Sydney put her hands on Abby's shoulders. "Abby, we aren't doing anything wrong," she assured her. "Abigail asked us to get the Kool-Aid. Abigail wants to dye her hair. Don't worry!"

Don't worry! thought Abby. *That's what everyone keeps telling me. Don't worry about the play. Don't worry about the boys. Don't worry about dying Abigail's hair.*

The car horn beeped.

"Come on," said Sydney. "Gram is waiting."

Abby walked out to the car and climbed in. She was sure that Gram could see the Kool-Aid packages bulging in her pocket. She sat down and fastened her seat belt. The paper packages crackled every time she moved.

Gram glanced in the rearview mirror. "I think it's very nice of you girls to spend so much time with Abigail," she said. "You probably brighten her day!"

Abby had a sudden vision of Abigail with bright pink hair. Sydney must have had the same idea because she started to giggle. Abby covered her mouth and looked straight ahead.

Gram dropped them off at the door of the nursing home. "I'll be back in about an hour," she said. "Call me if you need me sooner."

"Okay," said Abby. "Thank you!"

Abby stopped at the nurse's station when they went inside.

"Hi, girls," said Nurse Julie. "Did you come to see Miss Flynn?"

Abby nodded.

"I'm so sorry," Nurse Julie said. "She just left. She had a doctor's appointment this afternoon. They took her in the van."

Abby gulped. "Is she sick?" she asked anxiously.

"It's just a checkup," said Julie. "Abigail is very healthy for her age."

"Can we wait for her?" asked Sydney.

Julie looked at her watch. "Well, you can wait if you want to. But it's probably going to be at least an hour and a half. They just left about fifteen minutes ago."

Sydney looked at Abby.

"I don't know what to do," said Abby. "Gram was just going to the post office and the farmers market. She won't be gone very long."

"Could we leave Abigail a note?" Sydney asked.

"Of course," said Julie. She handed Sydney a tablet and a pen. "You can go back and leave it in her room if you want."

"Okay," Sydney said. Abby and Sydney ran down the hall to Abigail's room. It seemed very empty without Abigail there. Abby missed her smiling face.

"What should we say?" Sydney asked. "Should we leave the Kool-Aid or take it with us? What if someone finds the Kool-Aid or reads the note before Abigail comes back?"

"We'll have to write our message in code," Abby said. "We want Abigail to understand it but we don't want anyone else to."

"So we can't say that we are leaving her some Kool-Aid to dye her hair," said Sydney.

Abby rolled her eyes. "No," she said. "We need to hide the Kool-Aid."

Abby thought for a minute. She pulled the packages of Kool-Aid out of her pocket. "Give me your Kool-Aid," she said.

Sydney handed her packages to Abby. Abby took all of the Kool-Aid and pushed it under Abigail's pillow. Then she took the pen and pad from Sydney and wrote her message.

Sydney started to giggle when she saw what Abby had written. Abby tore off the note and laid it on the night table. The note said, *Sweet dreams, Abigail! Love, Abby and Sydney!*

Abby's Great Idea

The last rehearsal for the play was Saturday afternoon. Mrs. Mackenzie had the kids run through it twice. It wasn't very good. Abby forgot some of her lines and so did Sydney.

Mrs. Mackenzie laid her script on the table. "Why don't you kids take a break?" she suggested. "There are pretzels and lemonade in my office."

Abby's shoulders slumped. She looked at Sydney and stepped off the stage. "We stink!" she said. "Mrs. Mackenzie is just too nice to say it."

"There are just too many lines to remember," Sydney said. "It doesn't help that people keep stopping to watch either!"

Abby glanced at the group of library staff members sitting in the back row. "Maybe this is their lunch break," she said.

Dakota swaggered over. "Or maybe we are the best show in town!" he said.

Sydney rolled her eyes. "I guess you weren't listening then!"

"We are the *only* show in town," Abby replied. "But that doesn't make us any good. The play is two days away and we still don't know all our lines!"

"I know my part," said Zachary.

"You only have one line!" Abby protested. "I'm on stage the whole time and so is Sydney!"

"Ribbit," croaked Dakota, hopping across the stage toward them.

"Stay away from me, you little toad!" Sydney screeched.

Abby shook her head. "This is a mess. We are a mess! How are we going to pull this play together?"

"Let me know when you figure it out," said Zachary. "I'm going to go eat pretzels."

"Me too," said Dakota.

"Thanks a lot!" said Abby.

Mrs. Mackenzie put a hand on Abby's shoulder. "Could you girls help me get the props out of the cellar?"

"Sure," said Abby.

They followed her to the back of the library. The cellar steps were dark and dusty. A single lightbulb lit the stairway. Their shadows tiptoed down the steps in front of them.

Abby glanced around the cellar. The librarians stored so many things here. The walls were stacked with boxes, books, and newspapers.

"I think the boxes I want are over here," said Mrs. Mackenzie. She pointed at the wooden puppet theater in the corner. A stack of boxes were piled in front of it. Some boxes were marked *Christmas* in big red letters.

"This is so pretty," Abby said, running her hand along the side of the theater. "It looks like it should belong to a magician!"

The theater was painted blue with a row of gold stars along the top. It had two doors. A golden sun was painted on one door and a silver moon on the other.

"We haven't used it since last fall," said Mrs. Mackenzie. "I guess I buried it behind the Christmas decorations." She scooted the boxes over and opened the doors.

Abby peeked inside. "Wow!" she said. "It's a lot bigger than it looks!"

The top half of the back was open with a rod running across it.

Mrs. Mackenzie pointed out the wide shelf in the middle. "This is the puppet stage. I have the curtains in a box somewhere."

Abby noticed that the shelf stuck out at the back. "Why is there a shelf behind the curtain?" she asked.

"The puppeteers don't have to memorize their scripts," said Mrs. Mackenzie. "They put them on the shelf behind the curtain."

Abby looked at Sydney. She had a wonderful idea! "Mrs. Mackenzie," she asked, "could we use this puppet theater?"

"Sure," said Mrs. Mackenzie. "I'll get Art and Lois to bring it up to the program room after the Summer Reading Program is over."

"That's not what I mean," said Abby. "Could we use it today?"

Mrs. Mackenzie looked puzzled. "I don't understand. We can't put the

puppet theater up on the stage until the play is over."

Abby thought about all of Mrs. Mackenzie's puppets upstairs in the closet. "We have a king, a princess, and a frog puppet. Couldn't we turn the play into a puppet show, instead?" she asked. "Our scripts would be right in front of us. Then we wouldn't forget our lines."

Sydney clapped. "That's an awesome idea!" she yelled.

Mrs. Mackenzie smiled. Glitter sparkled on her rosy cheeks. "I think you're right," she said. "That is an awesome idea!"

"But you're the narrator," said Sydney. "We don't have a narrator puppet."

"The narrator is just someone who tells the story," said Mrs. Mackenzie. "Abby can choose any puppet she wants to be the narrator."

Abby smiled. "I'll choose the monkey," she said. "He's always been my favorite!"

Pizza and Puppeteers

Dakota crouched on the stage looking up at Abby. "Don't I get to hop around anymore?" he asked.

Abby extended the frog puppet. "You won't be hopping, but you will be making your frog puppet hop," she explained.

"It will be fun!" said Sydney.

"Okay," said Dakota taking the puppet.

"You're still going to have to practice," said Mrs. Mackenzie. "You have to make your frog look believable on the stage."

Zachary picked up his puppet. "The king is awesome!" he said, patting the long, white beard into place.

"The princess is really beautiful," said Sydney. "I love her green velvet dress and her silver crown!"

Mrs. Mackenzie went to close the program room door. "Let's get started," she said. "We have a lot to do. We can use a folding table for a stage until Art can move the puppet theater upstairs."

The play went much better when Sydney and Abby could read their lines. Mrs. Mackenzie made suggestions about how to make the puppets' mouths move when they spoke. They even practiced bringing the puppets on and off stage and having them bow at the end.

Mrs. Mackenzie clapped her hands when they finished. "This is really good!" she said. "It's cute and funny! All of you did a really great job!"

Abby grinned. She didn't need to worry about forgetting her lines anymore. Now, she was looking forward to being in the play!

Then Art and Lois arrived with the puppet theater. They brought it in on a big cart and set it up on the stage. Cobwebs hung in some of the corners and dust covered the blue paint.

"I can help clean the puppet theater," Abby offered. "It's pretty dirty."

"We'll have to do it today," Mrs. Mackenzie said. "The play is Monday night and the library isn't open tomorrow."

"That's okay," said Abby. "Gram told me I could stay as long as you needed me to."

"I can stay, too," said Sydney. "I'm sleeping at Abby's house tonight."

Mrs. Mackenzie smiled. "Thank you so much!" she said.

The boys looked at each other and headed for the door.

"See you Monday," said Zachary.

"Bye," said Dakota.

Abby sighed as the door closed. "Remember when we used to all help Mrs. Mackenzie together?" she said to Sydney. "The boys haven't been here very much since they dyed your hair."

"Maybe they think you are still mad at them," said Mrs. Mackenzie.

"I'm not mad anymore," said Sydney. "It wasn't a nice thing to do, but the pink color is almost gone. They just better not do it again. If I want to dye my hair, I'll do it myself!"

"Dakota told me they were sorry," said Abby. "I just wish things could be back the way they were."

"Me too," said Sydney.

Mrs. Mackenzie got a bucket of soapy water and some cloths. Abby and Sydney started to wipe the dust off the puppet theater. The sun and moon sparkled as the cloths moved back and forth. The blue paint looked bright and shiny again!

Mrs. Mackenzie smiled. "You girls are such a big help!" she said. "How would you like to have pizza for supper?"

Sydney and Abby looked at each other. "We love pizza!" they both said.

Just then, the program room door opened. Zachary and Dakota stepped inside.

"Sydney, we want you to know we are very sorry. We'd like to stay and help," said Dakota. "Can I call my dad?"

"Sure," said Mrs. Mackenzie. "You can use the phone in my office."

"I am sorry, Sydney. I'll call, too," said Zachary. "I think we should all help!"

Mrs. Mackenzie winked at the girls. "I guess I should order lots of pizza!" she said. "The Book Bunch is back on the job!"

Claim to Fame

Abby peeked from behind the puppet theater. Tonight was their big performance! The room was already filled with people. Mrs. Mackenzie was smiling and shaking hands at the door.

"Why isn't anyone sitting in the front row?" whispered Abby.

"There's a reserved sign," said Dakota. "Mrs. Mackenzie put it there."

"Maybe our parents are supposed to sit in the front row," suggested Zachary.

"My parents are sitting over there," Abby said, pointing at a row about halfway back.

Abby slipped the monkey puppet on her hand. Its fur felt soft and warm. She practiced opening and closing his mouth. Her script lay on the shelf in front of her. She was ready to start!

Zachary grabbed Abby's arm. "Is that Abigail Flynn?" he asked. "Look at her hair!"

Abby and Sydney leaned around the corner of the theater. The front row was

full of residents from Evergreen Nursing home. Abigail's hair was bright pink! The other residents had blue, purple, green, and red hair!

Sydney giggled. "She must have shared her Kool-Aid! That's why the first row was reserved. They must have asked for front-row seats!"

Abby laughed, too. "They look so cute!" she said. "I'm so glad they came!"

"We have to do a really good job," said Sydney, looking at the boys. "No more jokes. Just follow your scripts!"

Dakota waved the frog puppet in the air. "I'm ready!" he said.

"Me too," said Zachary as he held up the king.

Soon, it was time to start. Abby had butterflies in her stomach. She was excited, but she wasn't scared. She was so glad to have her script right in front of her.

"Welcome to our Summer Reading Finale," said Mrs. Mackenzie. "Tonight we will give some prizes and we'll have some great refreshments. But first, I have a special treat. I'd like to present Evergreen Library's puppet play, *The Princess and the Frog*!"

The audience clapped and then everything got very quiet. Mrs. Mackenzie walked behind the puppet theater. She nodded to Abby.

Abby cleared her throat. She slid the monkey puppet under the curtain and began. "Once upon a time there was a beautiful princess."

The play went perfectly. No one forgot any lines! People laughed at all the right spots. The audience clapped and clapped when Abby, Sydney, Dakota, and Zachary came out with their puppets at the end. Mrs. Mackenzie made them all take a bow.

Abby and Sydney ran to give Abigail Flynn a hug when they were finished.

Abigail squeezed both of them. "The play was wonderful!" she said. "You girls did such a good job! I'm so proud of you!"

Abby blushed. "Thank you," she said.

"And Gram arranged to have the van bring us to see it!" Abigail added. "Wasn't that nice?"

"It was very nice," said Abby. She smiled at Gram. "Maybe Mrs. Mackenzie would let us borrow the puppets sometime. We could come to the nursing home and put on a play there."

"That would be wonderful!" said Abigail. "Not everyone was able to come tonight."

"Your hair looks beautiful!" said Sydney.

Abigail patted her hair into place. "When everyone saw my hair they wanted to dye theirs, too," she said. "We used all the Kool-Aid. But I'm the only one with pink hair. That's my claim to fame!"

Sydney twirled a lock of hair around her finger. "My color is starting to wash out," she said. "I guess I don't have a claim to fame anymore."

Mrs. Mackenzie walked up just then. She put her arms around Sydney and

Abby. "Your claim to fame is that you are wonderful puppeteers!" she said. "I am so proud of both of you!"

"I really had fun!" Abby said. "I love doing puppet shows!"

"Me too," said Sydney. "Can we do another one next year?"

Mrs. Mackenzie laughed. Glitter twinkled on her hair and face. "Of course," she said. "Why should we wait until next year? Let's do one next month at Evergreen Nursing Home."

"Awesome!" said Abby and Sydney.

Abigail clapped her hands. "That is the best idea yet!" she said.

Puppet Shows

Puppet shows are a great way to participate in theater even if you get stage fright. Puppeteers stand behind a curtain and are not usually seen by the audience. They are often able to keep their scripts with them. Here are some things to remember when you are using puppets.

- Most school and public libraries own puppets. Some libraries run puppet workshops in the summer.

- Remember that your puppet is the actor when it is onstage. Have your puppet interact with other puppets even when it isn't speaking.

- Speak in front of a mirror. Practice opening and closing your puppet's mouth when your mouth moves.

- Make your puppet look natural. Keep its feet touching the stage when it is walking or standing.

- It is hard for puppets to carry things. Use as few props as possible in puppet plays.

- Practice different emotions with your puppet. Make it look sad, angry, or happy.

- Choose a voice for your puppet. A mouse might have a squeaky, little voice, but an elephant should have a strong, loud voice.

- Try writing plays for your puppets once you are comfortable using them. Include a beginning, a middle, and an end for your play.

- Have fun!